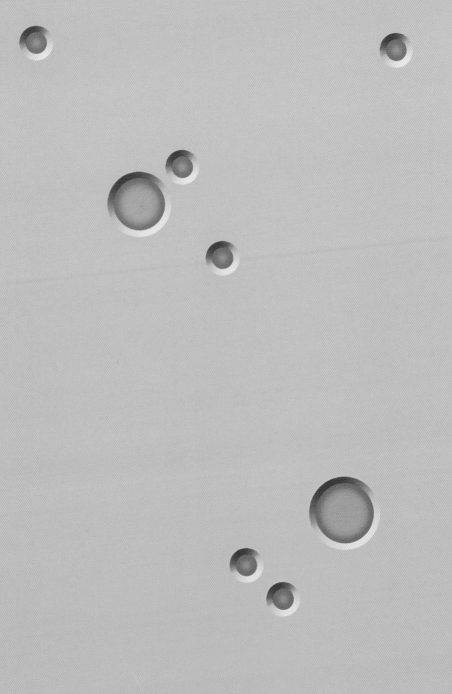

DAD AND I TURN INTO MICE

Written by **Mei Zihan**

Illustrated by **Bu Jiamei**

CARDINAL MEDIA

Mom always asks me, "Can you be quieter?"
But her voice is loud when she says it.

When I play in my room, she asks,
"Can't you be quieter?"

How can I bounce a ball without
making any noise?

When I put my bowl down, she asks,
"Can you be a bit quieter?"

When my chair knocks the table, she asks,
"Can you please be more quiet?"

I think my mom would like it if I were a mouse.

Then she wouldn't have to tell me to be quiet all the time.

I shut my eyes tightly and make a BIG wish:
"I want to be a mouse!"

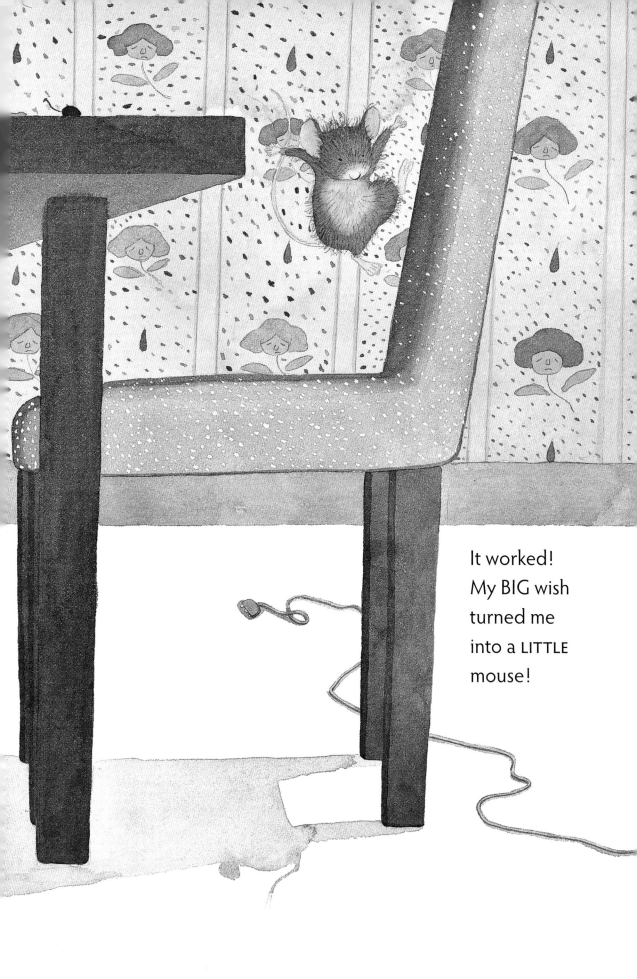

It worked!
My BIG wish
turned me
into a LITTLE
mouse!

I'm so little and quiet that Mom can't hear me.

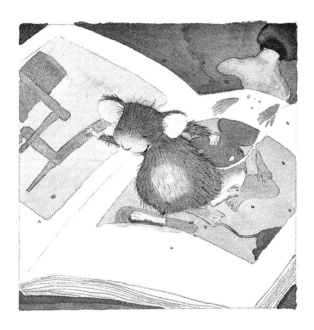

I can run around and be as loud as I want!

When Dad comes home, he sees me and says,
"Oh, no! We have a mouse in the house!"

No one knows it's really me! I make another
wish—and become a boy again.

"Where did you come from?" he asks.

I laugh and laugh. "I was the mouse!"

"Why were you a mouse?" asks Dad.

"Because when I am a little mouse, Mom doesn't have to tell me to be quiet all day," I say.

Dad says, "What a good idea. When I was your age, my mom told me to be quiet all the time, too. Why didn't I think to become a mouse?"

"Why don't you turn into a mouse now?" I ask.

And POOF! He does!

I turn back into a mouse, too.

Being mice is so much fun! We can laugh and run and play, and no one thinks we're too loud.

But Mom is worried about me.
It has been too quiet!

So Dad climbs right up next to
her ear and tells her our secret.
"We are mice so we can be loud!"

Mom surprises us by saying, "I understand. It's fun to be loud sometimes. When I was small, my mother always asked me to be quiet, too. I never thought to turn into a mouse."

"Please become a mouse with us," I say.

And POOF! She does!

Mom and Dad and I laugh and run and play and have a wonderful time.

I guess everybody needs to be a little loud sometimes!

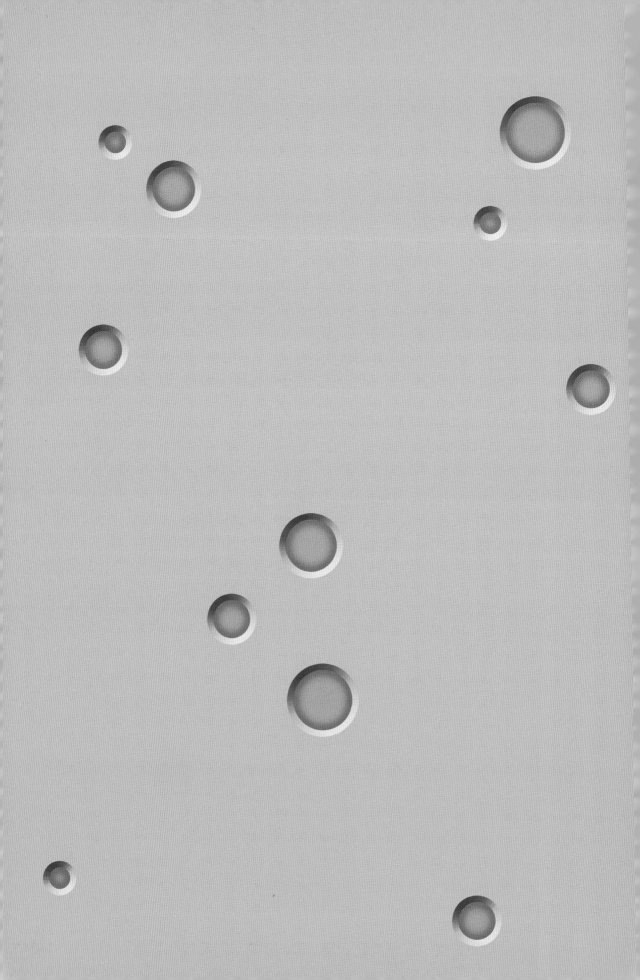